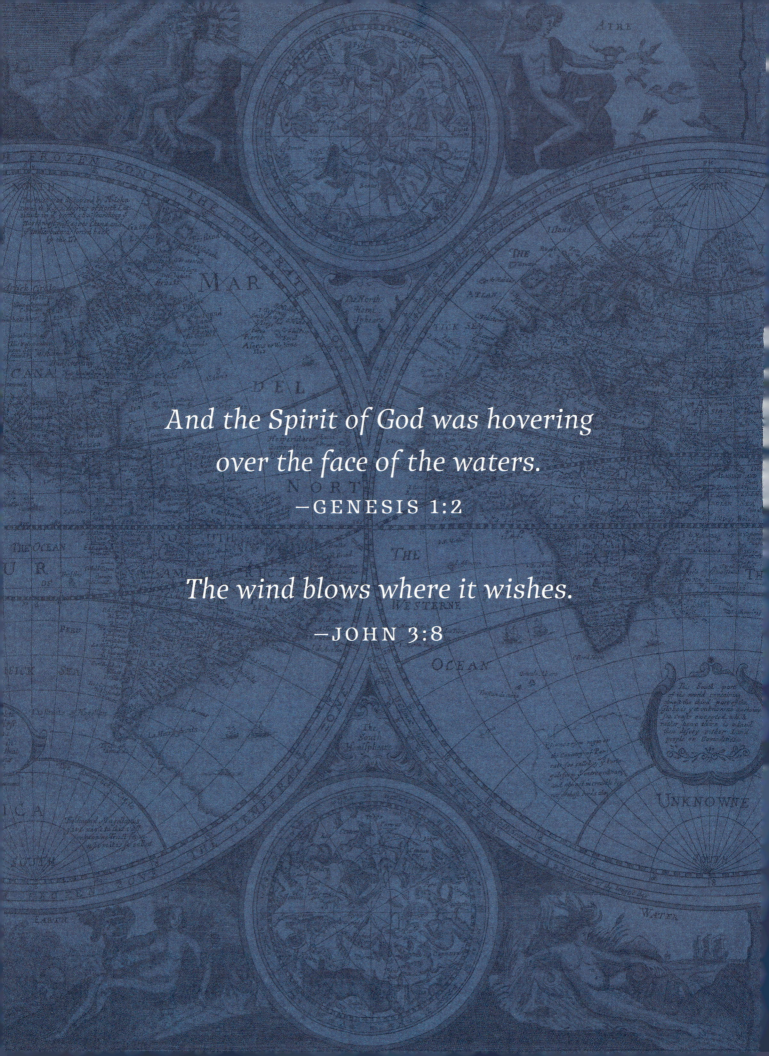

And the Spirit of God was hovering
over the face of the waters.
—GENESIS 1:2

The wind blows where it wishes.
—JOHN 3:8

Gaelan Gilbert

Illustrated by Ned Gannon

ANCIENT FAITH
PUBLISHING

CHESTERTON, INDIANA

Laurel grew up on a sailboat, amidst islands of trees
that came down to the edge of the windy sea.

She had always been on the boat,
and she had always been in the wind.

Sometimes the wind blew
from the north, and it was wet and cold.

Sometimes it blew from the south, and it was dry and warm.

Sometimes at night the wind whispered gently through the portholes
and rigging, while tides lapped at the sides of the hull.

Sometimes the wind rushed and howled, as storms thrashed the
sea and snapped the sail back and forth with power!

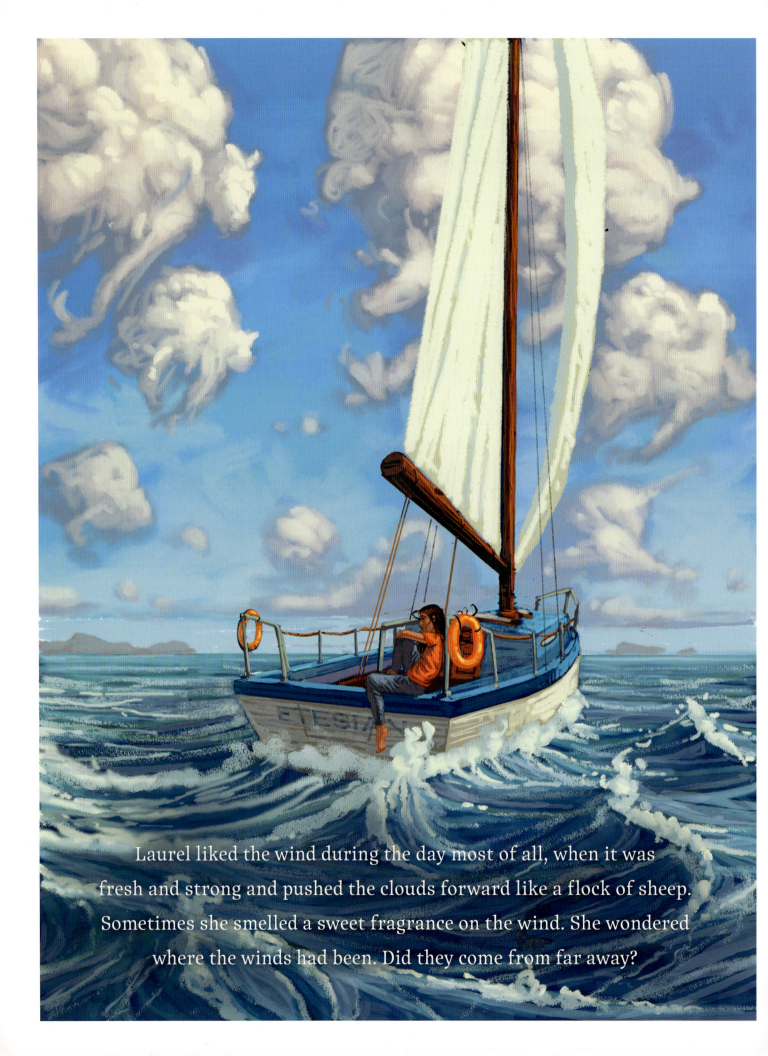

Laurel liked the wind during the day most of all, when it was fresh and strong and pushed the clouds forward like a flock of sheep. Sometimes she smelled a sweet fragrance on the wind. She wondered where the winds had been. Did they come from far away?

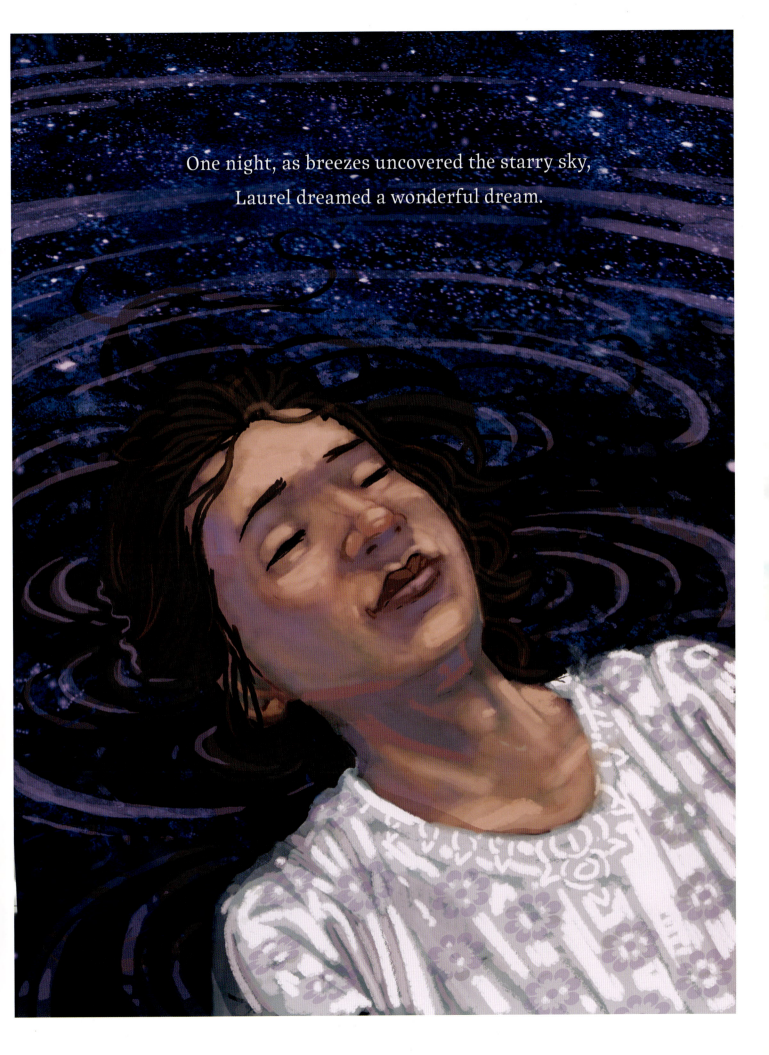

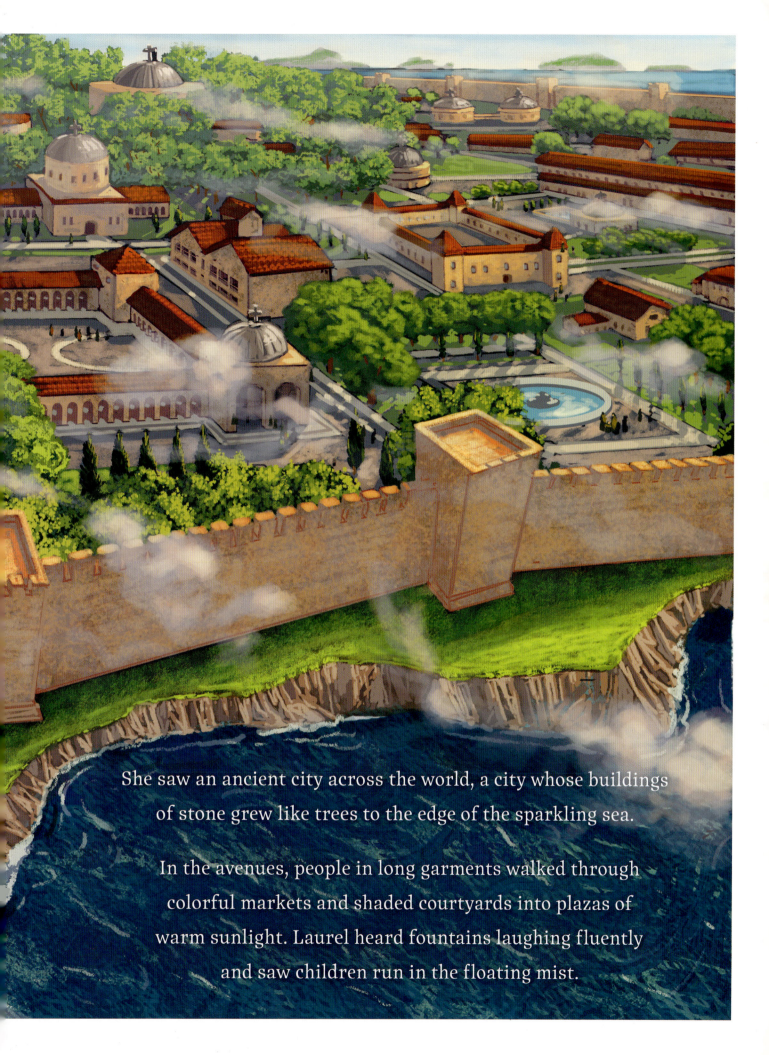

She saw an ancient city across the world, a city whose buildings of stone grew like trees to the edge of the sparkling sea.

In the avenues, people in long garments walked through colorful markets and shaded courtyards into plazas of warm sunlight. Laurel heard fountains laughing fluently and saw children run in the floating mist.

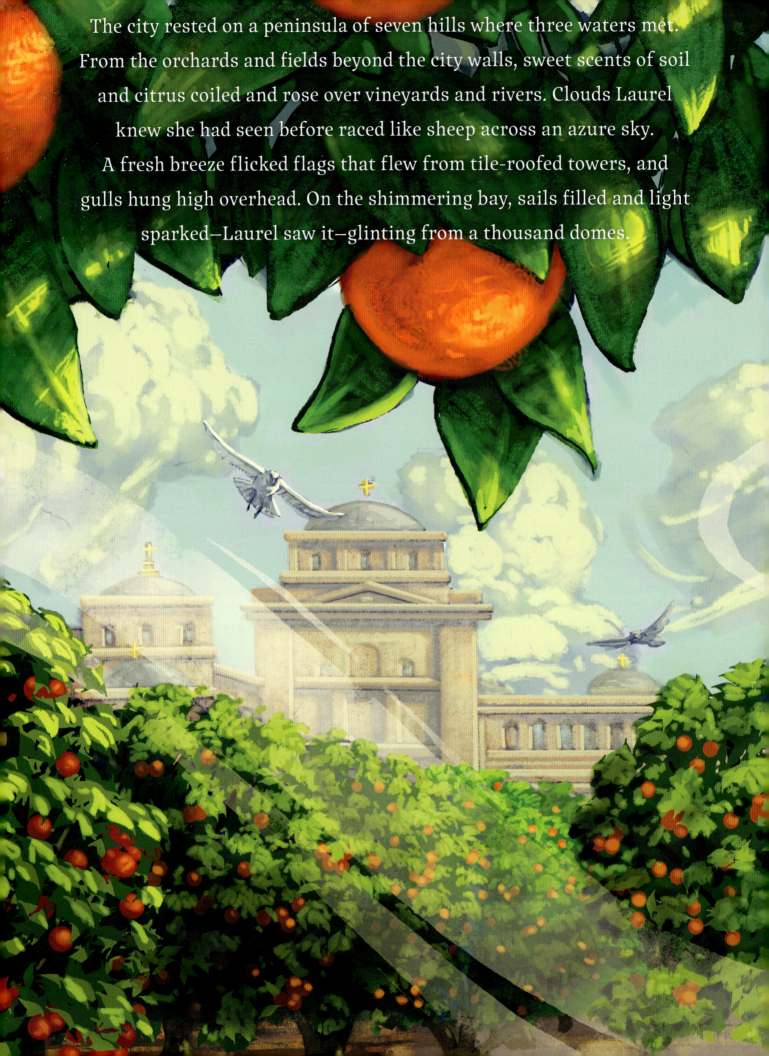

The city rested on a peninsula of seven hills where three waters met. From the orchards and fields beyond the city walls, sweet scents of soil and citrus coiled and rose over vineyards and rivers. Clouds Laurel knew she had seen before raced like sheep across an azure sky. A fresh breeze flicked flags that flew from tile-roofed towers, and gulls hung high overhead. On the shimmering bay, sails filled and light sparked—Laurel saw it—glinting from a thousand domes.

A steady breath blew fresh from the cold mountains of the north, through lush valleys in the east, up from southern sands, and across the middle sea, kissing Laurel's cheeks. The winds spun as three, then as one.

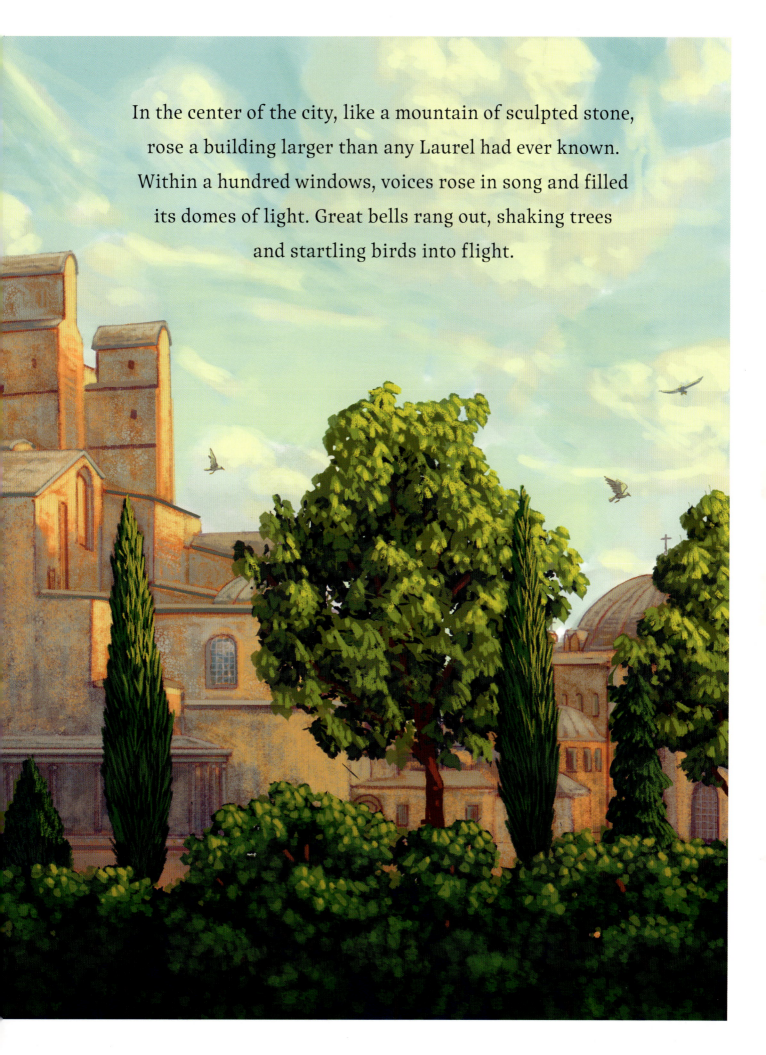

In the center of the city, like a mountain of sculpted stone, rose a building larger than any Laurel had ever known. Within a hundred windows, voices rose in song and filled its domes of light. Great bells rang out, shaking trees and startling birds into flight.

In a forest of marble pillars under a golden sky, Laurel saw a line of figures brightly robed processing to the altar, with candles, crosses, and censers billowing a sweet fragrance in the shafted light. A single voice then prayed, naming those who still breathe, and those who no longer do.

Laurel saw hands raise an aer-cloth up and up again,
air pulling the scent of bread and wine,
vestments rustling, wick-flames fluttering.

Suddenly, the wind rushed through branches of olive and oak on seven hills. She heard the wind in the leaves lift up its voice like many waters, streaming to the stars over the garden where God walked in the cool of the day.

Laurel looked up to see.
There—He walks and calls out for
lost Adam. After long lulled centuries,
He finds and awakens him from dying
dreams of dark bones and stone locked.

The Lord reaches across galaxies for Adam's hand.
Filling lungs, He bends low as a man and heaves up
all time from below, huffing a single breath as Hades exhales
a whimpering blast that flaps His white robe like a flag.

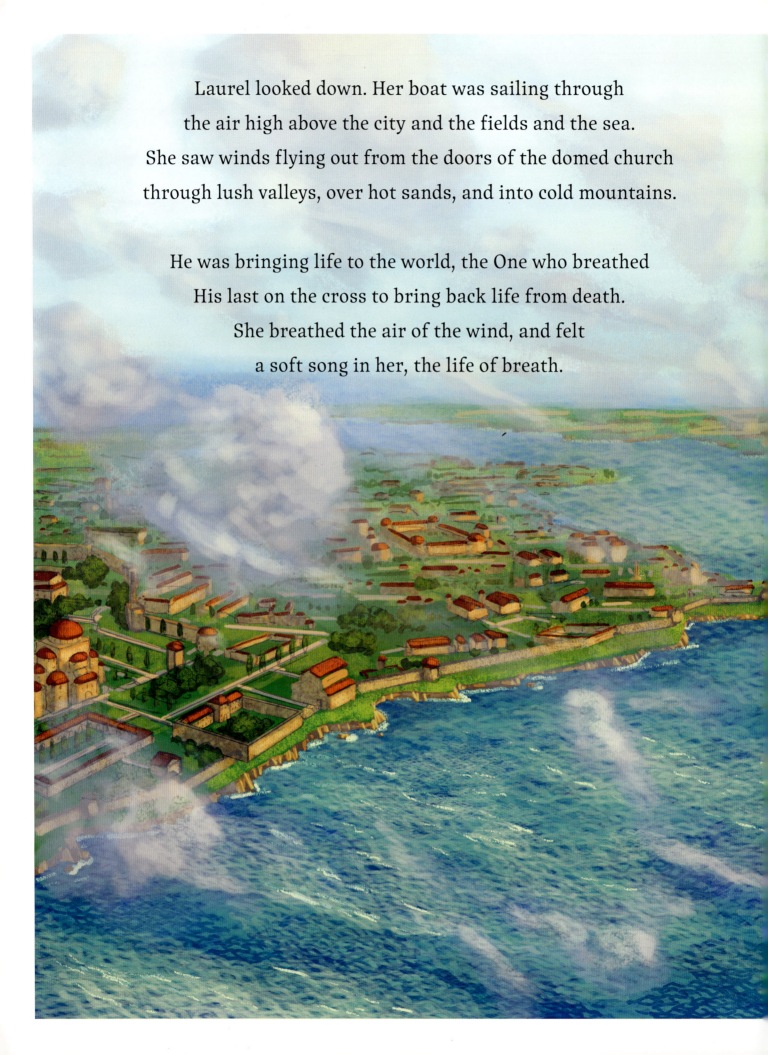

Laurel looked down. Her boat was sailing through
the air high above the city and the fields and the sea.
She saw winds flying out from the doors of the domed church
through lush valleys, over hot sands, and into cold mountains.

He was bringing life to the world, the One who breathed
His last on the cross to bring back life from death.
She breathed the air of the wind, and felt
a soft song in her, the life of breath.

Outside on the deck, Laurel smelled a sweet fragrance on the wind, as the morning sun rose to warm the waters and awaken the trees.

*For Mom—whose breathing was once my own.
Your love, laughter, and compassion for others first unlocked the doors
of faith in my soul. Through the breathtaking beauty of Orthodox
worship—in a land you traveled to first—the Lord opened them.
This book is for you.*
—GG

For Eliot and Claire and all daydreamers
—NG

Laurel and the Wind

Text copyright ©2020 Gaelan Gilbert • Illustrations copyright ©2020 Ned Gannon

All rights reserved.
No part of this publication may be reproduced by any means, electronic, mechanical, photocopying, recording, scanning, or otherwise, without the prior written permission of the publisher.

PUBLISHED BY:
Ancient Faith Publishing • A division of Ancient Faith Ministries
PO Box 748 • Chesterton, IN 46304

ISBN: 978-1-944967-71-0

Printed in China
store.ancientfaith.com

Library of Congress Control Number: 2020932161

GAELAN GILBERT

Gaelan Gilbert is a writer and teacher who has lived in California, Greece, Canada, and the American heartland. He received a PhD in English from the University of Victoria, BC, where he enjoyed studying alliterative dream-vision poems like *Pearl and Piers Plowman*. He has published scholarship in literary and theological studies, and also a collection of poems, *One Is Found First*.

Gaelan is the headmaster of Christ the Savior Academy in Wichita, KS, where he lives with his wife and family, and is a visiting professor of Arts & Humanities at the University of St. Katherine in San Diego, CA. *Laurel and the Wind* is his first children's book, and it began as a bedtime story for his children. Although currently living far from the sea, he sails whenever he can on a nearby lake in his daggerboard craft, *Sygny*.

NED GANNON

Ned Gannon earned a B.F.A. degree from the Kansas City Art Institute and an M.F.A. from the School of Visual Arts in New York. His art has been recognized by the Society of Illustrators in New York and the Society of Illustrators in Los Angeles, as well as the *Communications Arts* juried "Illustration Annual."

His work has been exhibited or represented in collections in fourteen countries. He has works in the permanent collection of Isle Royale National Park and the Staten Island Museum in New York. He lives in Wisconsin with his wife, two kids, and his adopted dog, Storm.

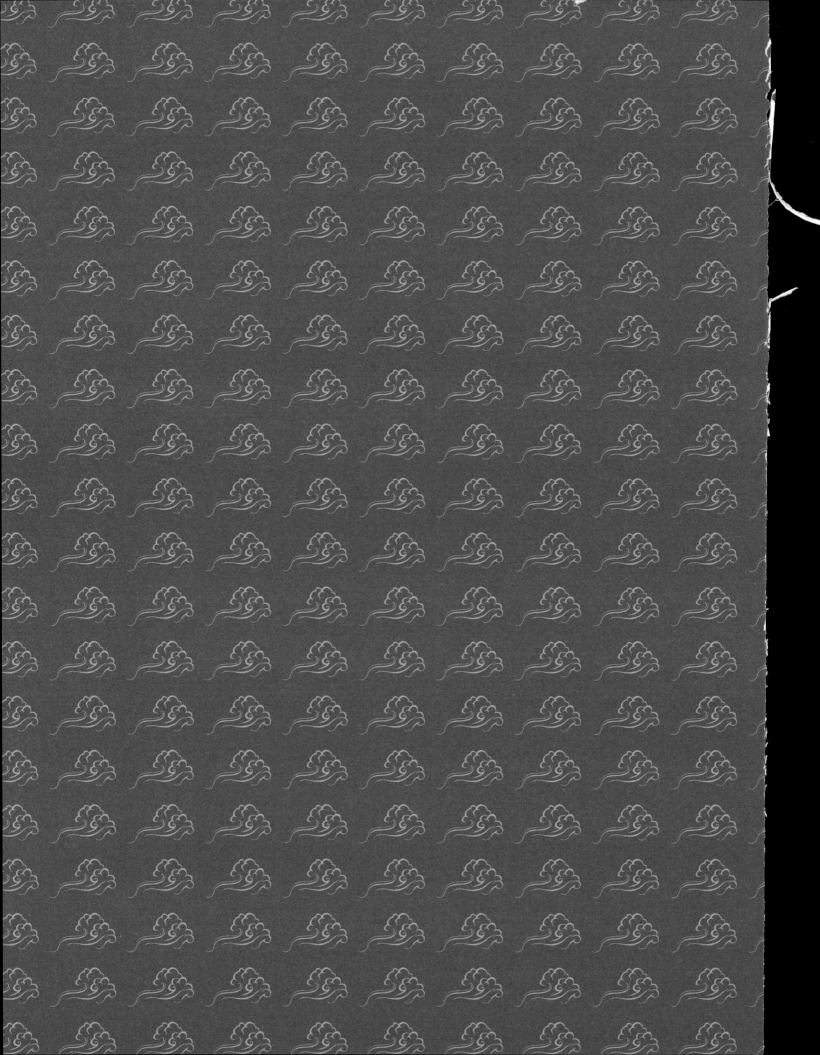